D1340539

hardie grant EGMONT

Volcanic Panic
first published in 2014
this edition published in 2017 by
Hardie Grant Egmont
Ground Floor, Building 1, 658 Church Street
Richmond, Victoria 3121, Australia
www.hardiegrantegmont.com.au

A CiP record for this title is available from the National Library of Australia.

Text copyright © 2014 H.I. Larry
Illustration and design copyright © 2014 Hardie Grant Egmont

Illustrations by Craig Phillips
Illustrations inked by Latifah Cornelius
Design by Simon Swingler

Printed in China through Asia Pacific Offset.

1 3 5 4 2

VOLCANIC PANIC
BY H.I. LARRY

ILLUSTRATIONS BY CRAIG PHILLIPS

hardie grant EGMONT

CHAPTER

It just isn't fair, thought Zac Power as he stared at the page in front of him. *I'm a secret agent! Why am I stuck here learning fractions?*

It was almost the end of a long school day, and Zac was counting down the minutes to the bell.

He may have been a highly trained member of the Government Investigation

Bureau, but that was all top secret. As far as his school was concerned, he was just an ordinary kid.

Zac's teacher, Mrs Tran, was away that day. They had a substitute teacher taking their class. Usually that was great because it meant the class got to do lots of fun stuff like art and PE.

But not this time. This new teacher had made them sit at their desks all day doing maths worksheets until Zac thought his brain would melt.

The new teacher's name was Ms Sharpe. She was tall and thin, and her jet-black hair was streaked with blue.

Zac didn't like her. There was something

about her smile that made Zac feel like he was in trouble, even though he was sure he hadn't done anything wrong. Not today, anyway.

Finally, the bell rang. Zac stuffed the worksheets into his maths book and got up to leave with the rest of the class.

'Just a minute please, Zac,' called Ms Sharpe. 'I need to rush off to an important meeting. Could you please close the blinds before you go?'

Zac sighed and walked back across the classroom towards the windows. He was about to pull the blinds down when suddenly, out of the corner of his eye, he saw something red and gleaming.

Sitting outside on the windowsill was a rock. It was about as big as Zac's hand, and it was glowing like it had just shot out of a volcano.

Zac looked around cautiously, but Ms Sharpe had disappeared.

His spy senses tingled. He opened the window and reached a hand out towards the rock.

For a moment, the rock burned red hot under his fingers. But then it grew cool and turned black.

A second later, the rock made a loud hissing sound and cracked open in Zac's hand, revealing a little silver disk. Zac's eyes lit up. *Excellent!*

A disk like this could mean only one thing – a new mission from GIB!

Zac smiled. His boring school day was about to get a whole lot more interesting.

CHAPTER

Zac raced to his schoolbag, and pulled out a small electronic tablet.

This was Zac's new SpyPad, the Pulsetronic V-66. It played video games, and it was also a phone, a code breaker, a laser, and just about everything else a spy could need.

Zac slipped the disk into his SpyPad.

CLASSIFIED
MISSION INITIATED 3 P.M.

GIB has received a distress call from Agent Hot Shot, who is stationed on a small volcanic island called the Isle of Magma.
Agent Hot Shock reposets that the island has become extremely active, and may erupt as soon as tomorrow afternoon. He needs immediate assistance.
A cloaked GIB jet is waiting for you behind the kindergarten cubby house.

YOUR MISSION
- Locate and rescue Agent Hot Shot.

~ END ~

Zac pulled the disk out of the SpyPad and pocketed it. Leaving his schoolbag under his chair, he dashed down the hall and raced outside.

The playground was crawling with kids and their parents. Zac knew he'd have to be careful not to let anyone see what he was doing.

He slowed down and walked the rest of the way to the cubby house at the far end of the playground.

Hang on, thought Zac as he neared the cubby house. *If the jet I'm looking for is cloaked, that means it's going to be invisible.*

How am I supposed to climb aboard a jet that I can't even see?

But Zac's question was answered a moment later when he slammed into something cold and hard. 'Ouch!'

The invisible jet was right there in front of him.

Well, Zac thought as he rubbed his throbbing head, *at least I found it.*

Now came the hard part. He had to find a way inside.

Zac stared at the empty space in front of him. He was suddenly reminded of something he'd learnt in science last term about bats using echolocation to find their way in the dark.

This gave Zac an idea. Peering around to make sure that no-one was watching, he set the laser on his SpyPad to Multi-Beam, and pointed it in the direction of the cloaked jet.

Several sharp green beams shot out of the SpyPad. The laser beam bounced off the jet in front of him, lighting it up around the edges.

Zac moved the laser across the body of the jet until he found the cockpit door. He turned off the laser, pulled on the door handle, and climbed aboard.

The cockpit of the jet was small and cramped, not at all up to GIB's usual standard. Everything inside was black, except for the gleaming blue control panel.

Before Zac had even had a chance to run a pre-flight check, the door hissed closed and the jet slowly rose into the air above the school.

Autopilot, Zac thought to himself. *Sweet!*

Zac sat back in the hard plastic seat and breathed a sigh of relief. He was finally on his way!

Even though his jet was speeding through the air, Zac knew that the trip to the Isle of Magma would probably take several hours. It wasn't long before he started getting bored.

At first, it had been kind of cool to watch the city down below. But Zac had been on heaps of jet flights before, and he got tired of sightseeing pretty quickly. Anyway, he was out over the open ocean now, and it was getting dark, so there wasn't a whole lot to see. For a while Zac passed the time playing games on his SpyPad, but after his tenth round of *Ninja Nightmare* even that got boring.

Zac glanced at his watch again, feeling impatient.

9.24 P.M

He wished that something would happen, just to break the boredom.

And at that moment, something did.

A face appeared on the screen of his SpyPad. It was Zac's older brother, Leon.

Like the rest of the Power family, Leon

worked for GIB. But Leon wasn't a field agent like Zac.

He worked on GIB technology, and was in charge of some of the cool spy gadgets that Zac and the other GIB agents used to complete their missions.

'Zac, where are you?' Leon demanded. 'You're in big trouble with Mum for not having swept the leaves up from the driveway. And it's already past your bedtime!'

'Where do you think I am?' said Zac, surprised. 'I'm on a mission!'

On the screen of the SpyPad, Zac noticed Leon's raised eyebrow. 'Mission? What mission?'

'The mission to rescue Agent Hot Shot from the Isle of Magma!' said Zac. He was starting to get annoyed. 'The mission you sent me on with the cloaked jet!'

'Zac, what are you talking about?' Leon asked. 'You haven't been sent on a mission. Nothing's come through from HQ all day.'

'But I found a disk at school and…' Zac trailed off as he realised what must have happened.

'The mission disk!' Zac cried, pulling the little silver disk out of his pocket. 'It's a fake!'

Now Leon looked worried. 'Zac, you've got to turn that jet around right now and come home.'

'Right,' said Zac quickly. He reached out and started tapping at the sea of blue buttons in front of him.

Nothing happened.

'I'm locked out,' Zac said, trying not to panic. 'Nothing's working! The whole control panel is locked.'

'OK, calm down,' said Leon. He didn't sound very calm himself. 'Just, um, sit tight for a minute. I'll see what I can do.'

On the SpyPad's screen, Zac could see his older brother tapping frantically at his keyboard. Leon was trying to over-ride the jet's computer.

Suddenly the image of Leon on the SpyPad began to flicker.

'Leon,' said Zac, 'you're breaking up!'

'I know,' said Leon, his fingers still flying across the keyboard in front of him. 'It looks like someone's trying to jam our signal. I think —'

But the screen blinked and flicked off. Leon was gone.

Zac pulled the handle of the cockpit door, but it was sealed shut.

Wherever this jet was headed, Zac Power was going with it.

And there was nothing he could do about it.

CHAPTER 3

I've got to get out of this jet! thought Zac, as he looked around for something to help him escape.

If this had been a real mission, Leon would have given him a bunch of cool new gadgets to get him out of every sticky situation. But now all he had were the contents of his pockets.

He had two sticks of ParaGum, but even if he could open the door, what good would it do to parachute down into the freezing ocean?

He also had a couple of Marble Flares, but right now a flash of blinding light would only make things worse.

And then of course he was wearing his Turbo Boots, which would have been great…except that he hadn't refuelled them all week. They probably only had one good jump left in them.

At least Zac wouldn't have to wait long to find out where he was going. Looking up, he spotted something red and glowing ahead.

It was the mouth of a volcano. An extremely *active* volcano. And he was headed straight for it.

As the jet flew closer, Zac saw that the volcano sat in the middle of a tiny tropical island. The whole place looked completely deserted.

The jet whooshed to a stop, hovering just above the mouth of the volcano. Lava splattered upwards and lashed the jet on all sides.

After a few moments, a loud siren sounded and the jet began moving again.

Zac's heart skipped a beat. The jet was dropping. He was being flown down inside the volcano!

As the jet descended, Zac decided that he'd better be ready for anything. He pocketed the ParaGum and the Flare Marbles. Then he used the fake mission disk to back up the contents of his SpyPad, and slipped it inside his left sock.

Zac checked the time.

9.42 P.M

The jet plunged lower and lower, past brown rock and flowing lava, until it finally emerged into an enormous rocky cavern.

Zac blinked as he took in the sight. The cavern was filled with row after row of small black jets, at least fifty of them.

They were all identical to the one that Zac was sitting in.

That means there are lots of people down here, he thought.

Looking down, Zac saw streams of glowing red lava criss-crossing along the floor of the cavern, in between the black jets. The lava flowed through archways that had been dug out of the rock walls.

From where Zac was sitting, it looked like his jet was being lowered down into an enormous glowing spider web.

With a jolt, Zac's jet landed between two others. Steel hooks rose up from the ground and locked around the plane's undercarriage.

The cockpit door hissed open, and a wave of cool air washed over him.

Hang on, thought Zac. *Why is it so cold in here?* He was no scientist, but he was pretty sure volcanoes were supposed to be hot.

Zac jumped down to the floor. The cavern was eerily quiet, and his footsteps echoed loudly off the stone walls.

Then, in the distance, Zac heard hissing steam and whirring motors.

The sounds grew louder and louder until, finally, a line of three black vehicles whizzed through a tall stone archway.

The vehicles looked a bit like jet skis, but they were gliding down one of the lava channels on cushions of steam. A stream of icy water shot out of the back of each vehicle, propelling it forward.

The lava skis pulled to a stop, and two enormous women strode towards Zac out of the steam clouds. Both of them were dressed in matching black jumpsuits with a small lightning-bolt crest on the front.

Then a third woman stepped forward, wearing the same black uniform. She tossed back her shiny black hair.

Zac gasped. It was the substitute teacher, Ms Sharpe.

'Ah,' said Ms Sharpe with a cold smile. 'Zac Power. Welcome to BIG Central Command!'

CHAPTER 4

Zac stared at her. He'd heard of awful teachers, but this was ridiculous.

Ms Sharpe, a BIG spy?

BIG spies were the most evil in the business. They were GIB's greatest enemies. It seemed like every week there was some crazy new BIG plot for Zac to deal with. And now here he was at their Central Command.

'So,' Zac said, putting on a brave face, 'this was the important meeting you had to rush off to?'

'Glad you could make it,' said Ms Sharpe with a smile. She gestured towards the two women beside her. 'Allow me to introduce my fellow BIG agents, Hunt and Sloane.'

She clicked her fingers and the two women advanced on Zac.

BIG is right, thought Zac. These women were gigantic! If not for their uniforms, they might have been mistaken for a pair of gorillas.

Zac tried to dodge, but the big women were surprisingly quick. Hunt grabbed Zac around the shoulders, while Sloane snatched the SpyPad from his hand and tossed it to Ms Sharpe.

'Thank you, Sloane,' said Ms Sharpe, putting the SpyPad into her pocket. 'We can't have our hostage calling for backup now, can we?

'Now then,' she continued, 'I suppose you've already figured out why we've brought you here to Central Command, smart boy that you are.'

'If you think I'm ever going to join you…' Zac began angrily, but Ms Sharpe cut him off with a cold laugh.

'No, no, boy. We're not interested in you at all. What we want is money, and lots of it.'

'Oh, right,' said Zac. 'The usual.'

'Yes, Agent Rock Star, the usual,' Ms Sharpe said. 'World domination is a costly business, you know I'm sorry to say that you have done a fine job of thwarting all of our past efforts to lay our hands on GIB's money.'

'Yeah,' said Zac, 'I have, haven't I?'

'Indeed,' said Ms Sharpe. 'But not this time.'

'Oh yeah?' said Zac. 'What's so different about this time?'

'This time,' Ms Sharpe said coolly, 'you are the one we're holding to ransom. That's why I've sent my daughter to deliver a message to your agency's headquarters.

Either GIB delivers 15 million dollars to us by midnight tonight, or they never see their favourite agent again.'

Zac's eyes dropped to his watch.

10.02 P.M.

That left him less than two hours to get out of here!

But my mission isn't supposed to finish until tomorrow afternoon, he thought angrily. Then again, he should have known BIG would pull something like this.

'Wait a minute,' said Zac, playing for time. 'Did you say your *daughter?*'

'That's right,' said Ms Sharpe. 'Come to think of it, I believe you've met my darling daughter Caz before.'

Of course, groaned Zac.

Caz Rewop was another dangerous BIG agent. Zac had met her several times. She'd left him stranded inside a collapsing pyramid, had tried to brainwash him, and had even had a crack at infiltrating GIB Headquarters.

'Yes, my dear Caz gathered all kinds of information for me while she was working undercover at GIB,' said Ms Sharpe, 'including the designs for your mission disks.'

So that's how they made the fake disk, Zac realised.

It was time to make a move. Without a second's warning, Zac twisted under

Hunt's grip and slipped a hand into his pocket. Closing his eyes tight, he pulled out a Marble Flare and threw it to the ground.

The marble shattered, sending out a flash of blinding light.

'Argh!' shouted Hunt.

Zac felt her hands loosen their grip, and he wrenched himself free.

Opening his eyes, Zac saw that all three BIG agents had been blinded by the flare.

They were now staggering around, blinking madly and snatching at the air in front of them.

Zac sprinted across the cavern in the direction of the lava skis.

'He's getting away!' yelled Sloane. 'After him!'

'Fool!' came Ms Sharpe's reply. 'You can't even see! You'll run straight into the lava! Let the boy run, he's got nowhere to go.'

Zac leapt onto one of the lava skis, brought it around and with a burst of steam, shot through the nearest archway and out of the cavern.

CHAPTER 5

Zac zoomed on the lava ski down the channel of molten rock. He knew he needed a way to contact GIB for help.

More archways rushed by on his left and right, each one opening up into another cavern.

But every room was crawling with more BIG spies. There were hundreds of them, sitting at computers, watching surveillance screens, testing gadget prototypes.

As long as he was hidden by the cloud of steam from the lava ski, Zac thought he was probably pretty safe. But he couldn't just keep on riding up and down the corridors forever.

What I need, Zac decided, *is a disguise.*

He continued cruising down the lava stream, his eyes peeled.

Then he saw it – a little archway coming up on his left, with a sign above that read LAUNDRY.

At that moment, as Zac glanced down at the controls of the lava ski, a slight problem occurred to him.

Where on earth are the brakes on this thing?

The laundry room was coming up too fast!

Zac took a deep breath, and jumped off the lava ski, landing on a narrow stone ledge.

Up ahead, the unmanned lava ski flew out of control and smashed up into the side of the corridor, shattering a big glass pipeline that ran down the rock wall.

KER-SMASH!

Oops! thought Zac, as a torrent of water burst out from the shattered pipe. Panicked shouts echoed out from rooms nearby.

Zac ducked through the archway into the laundry room and held his breath.

'It must be Rock Star!' called a woman from down the corridor. 'He's escaped – Sharpe just sent out an alert! Quickly, this way!'

Moments later, half a dozen BIG spies ran past the laundry room archway and down the corridor.

When they were gone, Zac breathed a sigh of relief.

Digging through a nearby laundry basket, Zac found a BIG jumpsuit that was about his size.

Zac quickly realised it must have been the dirty laundry basket. And the suit belonged to a pretty stinky BIG agent. But there wasn't a whole lot of choice.

Zac slipped the suit on over his own clothes, and headed out into the hall.

After wandering the walkways for about 20 minutes, his eyes down to avoid attention, Zac heard a weird chugging sound coming from a room up ahead.

Looking around to make sure the coast was clear, he slipped inside to investigate.

The noise turned out to be coming from a big, bulbous pumping machine that looked like a giant mechanical spider. Huge glass pipes stretched out from each side of the machine. The pipes ran along the walls and back out the archway.

I must have smashed one of those pipes with the lava ski, Zac thought.

As Zac watched, the machine sucked up streams of brown, steaming water from the four pipes on the left, and then pumped clear, icy water out through the four pipes on the right.

So the pipes run through this whole place, thought Zac. *And all that cold water must be what keeps this place from burning up.*

Zac glanced around the rest of the room until he finally found what he was looking for – a deserted computer workstation.

He reached down into his sock and pulled out the disk that he had stashed there earlier.

Slotting the disk into the computer, Zac uploaded his SpyPad's communication software. His hands fumbled with the unfamiliar keyboard, trying to get the keys to work.

At last, the screen flickered and Leon's face appeared.

'Leon!' Zac hissed, keeping his voice low. 'I need your help. I'm at BIG Central Command and –'

'I know,' Leon interrupted. 'We got the ransom note about an hour ago. We've got a team working on tracking you down. But Zac, this is huge! BIG Central Command! GIB has been trying to find that place for years!'

Zac looked at his watch.

10.51 P.M.

'Yes, yes, it's all very exciting,' he said impatiently, 'but right now I wouldn't mind a hand escaping!'

'Right,' said Leon, and Zac could see him tapping on his keyboard. 'Hang on a minute, I might be able to use your connection to interface with the BIG network.'

'OK, cool,' said Zac, glancing back over his shoulder.

There was still no-one coming, but he probably didn't have much time.

'Wow,' said Leon, his eyes lighting up, 'this is an incredible system! I've never seen network security this advanced before! The encryption protocols they've put in place here are really –'

'Not now, Leon!' said Zac. Only his brother could get excited about computer security at a time like this.

'Right,' said Leon. 'Working on it.'

A second later, there was an electrical crackling. Then the lights in the room dimmed.

'Leon, was that you?'

'Yeah,' said Leon. 'At least, I think it was. I've sent through a virus to knock out the security cameras and the phone lines. That should keep you safe for a while. Now all you have to do is – whoa!'

'What?' said Zac.

'Nothing,' said Leon quickly.

'Leon!'

'Really, it's nothing,' said Leon. 'It's just that the volcano you're in is very… active.'

'I know,' said Zac. 'It was spitting lava when I got here.'

'That was nothing,' said Leon. 'BIG has set up a massive wall of electricity at the base of the volcano. Right now, that force field is holding back the worst of the lava flow. But if anything went wrong with the force field, the eruption would probably –'

'Blow the whole island apart!' Zac finished for him, a plan forming in his mind. 'Excellent!'

'What?' said Leon, sounding alarmed. 'Zac, no! It's too dangerous!'

But Leon was suddenly drowned out by a shout and the sound of approaching footsteps.

'Got to go!' said Zac, pulling his disk from the computer. The screen flickered out, just as Ms Sharpe and her bodyguards appeared in the doorway.

CHAPTER 6

'Hi,' said Zac, standing up. 'I was just leaving.'

'Oh, no you weren't,' said Ms Sharpe.

Hunt and Sloane lunged forward, but this time Zac was ready for them. He dived quickly to the ground, ducking under Sloane's legs.

Zac rolled across the floor and got to

his feet again, reaching into his pocket and pulling out a stick of ParaGum. It seemed a shame to waste it like this, instead of floating away with it, but if his plan worked…

The enormous women hovered around Zac. But he stood his ground, chewing frantically. As they drew nearer, Zac started blowing.

'Chewing gum, Agent Power?' said Ms Sharpe, raising an eyebrow as Zac's bubble grew bigger and bigger. 'I've heard of staying cool under pressure, but this is –'

BANG!!

'Argh!' cried Hunt and Sloane together as the ParaGum bubble exploded across their faces.

Zac grinned, weaved his way around Ms Sharpe and ran out of the room. For the second time that night, Sharpe's goons were left staggering behind, rubbing blindly at their eyes.

Zac raced down the corridor, hard rock on one side, bubbling lava on the other, and Ms Sharpe hot on his heels.

They were heading deeper into the facility now. Instead of laboratories and computer workstations, Zac saw that the stone archways they were passing led into smaller rooms with beds, bookshelves and small black teddy bears.

Zac glanced over his shoulder as he sprinted around a corner. Ms Sharpe was gaining on him, a steely look in her eyes.

Looking up ahead again, Zac saw a big metal door coming up on his right.

Was it unlocked? Would he be able to open it?

Zac stopped at the door and wrenched frantically at its cold metal handle.

Come on, come on... Yes!

It took both arms to heave the door open. Zac dived inside and slammed the door shut behind him with an enormous crash of metal on metal. Then he threw down the deadlock.

He heard Ms Sharpe hammering furiously on the other side of the door, but she wasn't getting through in a hurry.

I'm safe for now, he thought, glancing at his watch.

11.08 P.M.

Zac had a look around the bedroom. *The bad news,* he thought to himself, *is that there doesn't seem to be another way out of here.*

Ms Sharpe had given up banging on the door, but all that meant was that she had probably gone for help.

He turned and looked around at the room he'd locked himself into. It was another bedroom, but this one was much nicer than the others he had just been running past.

There was an expensive-looking rug on the floor, a huge canopy bed at one end, and a wooden writing desk at the other.

Zac didn't have to look far to find out whose room he was in. There was an ID card and a little photo frame on the desk.

Smiling up at him from the picture frame were Ms Sharpe and her daughter, Caz. They were sitting on a park bench, eating ice-creams like a perfectly normal, non-evil mother and daughter.

Still, thought Zac, *there's something really creepy about that picture.*

'Zac! Hey, Zac!'

He jumped and spun around. *Where is that voice coming from?*

'Zac! Over here!'

Zac crossed over to the other side of the room, and then he saw it. Sitting on the end of Ms Sharpe's bed, blending in almost perfectly with the bedspread, was a shiny black iPod.

And it was talking to him.

CHAPTER 7

You've had a long day, Zac told himself sternly. *You've had a long, hard day, and now you're tired and you're imagining things. You know iPods can't talk.*

'Are you there, Zac?' said the voice.

'I know iPods can't talk!' Zac snapped.

And now you're arguing with a music player, thought Zac. *Fantastic.*

'What?' said the voice. 'Oh, right. No. Zac, it's me – Leon.'

'But –'

'Hold on a minute,' interrupted Leon, and a moment later his face appeared on the iPod screen.

'There we go.'

'Oh,' said Zac, finally catching on. 'But hold on. How are you doing that?'

'All the technology here is on a wireless network,' said Leon proudly. 'Including the iPods. Now that I've hacked into the system, I can pretty much go wherever I want.'

Zac grinned. For a nerd, Leon was pretty cool.

'Anyway,' Leon continued, 'I tracked the path of that jet you came in on, and used it to plot a course for the back-up team to come and rescue you. They're coming out in the Squid.'

'In the what?' said Zac.

'Oh, it's really cool!' said Leon excitedly. Clearly, the Squid was one of his own inventions. 'Wait until you see! Anyway, the back-up team is almost there, so all you need to do is get back out of the volcano and —'

'I can't leave yet,' said Zac. 'I still need to bring down the force field and destroy this place!'

'No, you have to get out of there!' said

Leon. 'I don't like BIG any more than you do, but it's too dangerous.'

'Leon, I can do this!' said Zac, almost shouting now. 'Look, there are plenty of jets up there for everyone to get away in. No-one will get hurt. All I have to do is stop BIG from using this place for evil.'

Leon sighed. 'I can't talk you out of this, can I?'

'No,' said Zac simply, 'you can't. Now, are you going to help me find the force field or aren't you?'

'Honestly,' Leon muttered as he went to work at his keyboard, 'you're so annoying when you get like this.'

Zac just smiled to himself.

'OK,' said Leon after a few moments, 'I have good news and bad news.'

Zac sighed. *Why is there always bad news?*

'The good news,' Leon continued, 'is that you won't have to go far to find the door that goes to the force field generator.'

'Great!' said Zac. 'Where is it?'

'You're standing on it.'

Zac stared down at his feet. Then he reached down and heaved aside the heavy rug, uncovering a little wooden trapdoor.

Well, thought Zac, *that explains why Ms Sharpe's bedroom needs a giant metal blast door.*

'Excellent!' said Zac. 'OK, what's the bad news?'

'The bad news,' said Leon, 'is that there

are about 20 BIG agents on the other side of that bedroom door, and they're approximately 30 seconds away from breaking it down.'

CHAPTER 8

BANG!

Zac's ears rang as something large and heavy crashed into the other side of the big metal door, shaking it on its hinges.

Time to go, thought Zac. He slipped the iPod into his pocket and bent down to grab hold of the brass handle at the edge of the trapdoor.

BANG!!

The whole room shook as Ms Sharpe and the other BIG agents took another shot at the door.

Zac tugged at the handle and the trapdoor lifted up easily, revealing a narrow, pitch-black tunnel. He bent down to peer inside, but couldn't see a thing.

BANG!!!

Zac looked back over his shoulder. The door was beginning to buckle.

Ms Sharpe's voice rang out from the other side of the door. 'Almost in!'

I'm almost out, Zac thought to himself, pulling a Marble Flare from his pocket. He tossed the marble down through the opening in the floor, and a moment later the whole tunnel burst into light. Careful not to look directly at the flare, Zac could see a series of thin metal bars forming a ladder down into the tunnel.

He tested the top rung with his foot and began to climb down.

No sooner had Zac's head and shoulders bobbed down into the tunnel than –

BANG!!!!
KER-SMASH!

The giant metal door exploded out of its frame and came crashing down on top of the tunnel entrance.

'Told you,' said a small voice from Zac's pocket.

Zac kept climbing down, and soon he'd reached the bottom of the tunnel. Shielding his eyes from the Marble Flare still burning at his feet, he peered around.

Now where do I go?

He didn't have to look far. From the end of a tunnel to his right, Zac heard a distant crackle of electricity. He could also see bright flashes of red, blue and purple.

Zac raced down the tunnel, which turned out to be longer than it looked.

As he drew closer to the force field generator, the fierce electrical crackling grew louder and louder.

Finally, Zac emerged from the passageway into what turned out to be another enormous cavern, almost as big as the jet hangar at the volcano's entrance.

Zac's stomach plummeted as he looked up at the far wall of the cavern, and saw that it wasn't a wall at all. It was a surging sea of molten rock that extended for 50 metres in each direction.

The only thing stopping all that lava from spewing out and flooding BIG HQ was the paper-thin force field being projected across the cavern by a little generator in the corner. It was freaky. It was kind of like standing in front of one of those enormous shark tanks at the aquarium.

And here I am, about to break the tank's glass, Zac thought.

He glanced down at his watch.

11.53 P.M.

Not that the ransom deadline would matter if his plan worked.

Zac ran to the computer station. A giant sign was posted on the wall above it.

DANGER
FORCE FIELD GENERATOR

NO ACCESS.

This generator operates under a 5-minute emergency lock-down protocol. In case of emergency, agents will have 5 MINUTES to leave BIG Central Command.

Zac glanced down at the little touch screen on the side of the generator, then pulled the iPod out of his pocket.

'Leon!' he said. 'The generator is password protected! I need a code to shut it down!'

'Right,' replied Leon. 'I'm on it.'

But at that moment, Ms Sharpe burst into the room.

Zac spun around and peered down the passageway behind her. 'Where's Hunt and Sloane this time?'

'Luckily for you, they were too, er, *big* to fit through the tunnel,' Ms Sharpe said.

I bet they were, thought Zac.

'Well, you'd better head back up there

yourself,' he said. 'In a few minutes, it's going to get pretty hot in here.'

Ms Sharpe laughed. 'I don't think so, Agent Rock Star. That generator is protected by state-of-the-art BIG security. There's not a spy in the world who could shut it down.'

DING!

A large blue button appeared on the touch screen and an electronic female voice could be heard over the crackling force field.

**PASSWORD ACCEPTED.
TOUCH SCREEN TO DEACTIVATE
GENERATOR.**

'Not a spy in the world,' said Zac proudly, 'except for my brother.'

Ms Sharpe looked like she'd just been punched in the stomach.

'Zac,' she said, sounding panicked, 'please, be reasonable! Let's talk about this like civilised people!'

'Right,' said Zac dryly, 'like the kind of civilised people who kidnap each other and trap them inside a volcano. I don't think so.'

He thrust out his hand toward the touch screen.

'WAIT!' cried Ms Sharpe.

Zac's finger froze, millimetres from the blue button.

'What?'

'Your grandfather!' Ms Sharpe said desperately, a mad gleam in her eye. 'I know you'd love to find him! I can help you. Come with me, Zac, and we'll find him together!'

For a long moment, the two agents stared at each other in silence. Zac's grandpa had disappeared on a jungle mission many years ago. Zac and his family had never heard from him since.

Then Zac broke the silence. 'My grand-father spent his life putting people like you out of business!'

And with that, he lifted his hand and slammed it down onto the touch screen.

'Time to move!' said Zac, and he bolted past Ms Sharpe and back through the passageway.

CHAPTER

WARNING: FORCE FIELD DEACTIVATION IN 5 MINUTES.

For a few seconds, Ms Sharpe stood frozen on the spot, staring at the force field. Then she turned on her heels and raced after Zac.

Reaching the end of the passageway, Zac clambered up the ladder and out into Ms Sharpe's bedroom.

Leaping over the battered metal door, he darted out of the room and back along the stony corridor.

Up ahead, BIG agents were streaming out into the corridor through the archways on either side, and sprinting off towards the jet hangar.

Zac could hear Ms Sharpe running behind him.

WARNING: FORCE FIELD DEACTIVATION IN 4 MINUTES.

Zac rounded another corner. Halfway down the corridor, he saw a lava ski lying abandoned on its side. He raced over, picked it up, and hoisted it down into the lava stream.

Hopping aboard, Zac took one last look around and saw Ms Sharpe staggering up the corridor, clearly out of breath.

WARNING: FORCE FIELD DEACTIVATION IN 3 MINUTES.

Zac sighed. Sometimes being a good guy was a pain in the butt.

'All right,' he said wearily, as Ms Sharpe caught up. 'Get on.'

'Huh?' she began. 'Why would you…?'

'Look, do you want to get out of here or not?' Zac snapped. 'Get on!'

Zac gave Ms Sharpe about three seconds to climb onto the lava ski behind him, then he gunned the accelerator. In a flurry of steam, they raced along the lava stream towards the hangar.

The lava ski bucked and bounced beneath Zac's feet and it took every ounce of his game-playing reflexes to keep it from spinning out of control.

WARNING: FORCE FIELD DEACTIVATION IN 2 MINUTES.

'That was a really nice thing to do,' Ms Sharpe said suddenly.

'What?' said Zac absently, struggling to control the speeding vehicle.

'Sharing your lava ski with me,' said Ms Sharpe, 'was a really nice thing to do.'

Zac rolled his eyes. 'Yeah? Well, lucky for you I'm the nice type.'

Zac sped around one final corner and

burst through the tall archway and out into the jet hangar.

'Jump!' yelled Zac, and he dived off the lava ski onto the stone floor. Ms Sharpe thudded to the ground next to him. A second later –

KER-SMASH!

The lava ski exploded against the cavern wall.

'Those things do have brakes, you know!' Ms Sharpe grunted.

'Right,' said Zac. 'Next time, you can be the driver and I'll be the evil kidnapper.'

Ms Sharpe moved to get up, but Zac stopped her with a look. 'I'll have my SpyPad back now,' he said, his hand out.

Ms Sharpe snarled and handed over the SpyPad.

WARNING: FORCE FIELD DEACTIVATION IN 1 MINUTE.

They leapt to their feet, looking around the enormous cavern. The same thought entered both of their heads.

Only one jet left. And there was no way both of them could fit inside.

'Take it!' said Zac.

'What?' said Ms Sharpe, as though she thought Zac was trying to lure her into some kind of trap.

'Take the jet!'

'But —'

'Ms Sharpe!' Zac shouted. 'You were a

lousy substitute teacher and you're an even lousier spy! The only way you're going to make it out of here is in that jet! Now get in there before I change my mind!'

Casting him one last suspicious look, Ms Sharpe bolted across the cavern and climbed up into the jet.

The cockpit door hissed closed and the sleek black aircraft rose quickly up through the volcano towards the safety of the open sky.

'OK,' Zac muttered to himself, 'time to get out of here.'

WARNING: FORCE FIELD DEACTIVATION IN TEN SECONDS.

Zac knew he had only one chance to escape.

NINE...

He ran across the floor of the cavern,

EIGHT...

leapt across the last lava stream in his path,

SEVEN...

positioned himself directly below the mouth of the volcano,

SIX...

crouched down on the ground,

FIVE...

pulled up the leg of his jeans,

FOUR...

reached for the green button on the side of his Turbo Boots,

THREE...

held his breath,

TWO...

and pushed the button.

ONE.

But absolutely nothing happened. *That's not good,* Zac thought as the whole cavern began to shake.

FORCE FIELD DEACTIVATED.

CHAPTER 10

He knew his Turbo Boots were running low on fuel, but surely they had enough in them for one more jump. He pressed the button quickly with his finger.

Suddenly, lava spewed into the hangar from all sides, gushing in through the stone archways and blasting them apart with the force. Waves of molten rock swept across the floor of the hangar, melting everything in their path.

In seconds, the whole cavern would be a swirling ocean of fire, and Zac would be in it. The waves were only metres from him now. Only centimetres. Then —

KA-BLAM!

The twin rockets in his Turbo Boots roared to life, and he was thrown upwards.

He was tearing his way up through the throat of the volcano now, racing past the rock walls at an insane speed.

Zac looked down and saw hot lava rushing up below. The rockets in his shoes sputtered as the Turbo Boots ate up the last of their fuel.

Come on, come on! Zac thought, willing the boots to keep going. *Almost there!*

And then he was clear. Zac leant forwards and the rockets propelled him out over the ocean.

A moment later, the volcano erupted into fire and ash. *Now that,* Zac thought to himself, *was a close one.*

Then, with a final splutter, the Turbo Boots gave out and Zac began falling towards the dark sea.

Zac reached into his pocket and snatched up the last piece of ParaGum. Then he crammed it into his mouth, and chewed as hard as he could.

He was tumbling head over heels

through the air now, towards the churning ocean below.

Sticking out his tongue, Zac blew into the ParaGum with all his might.

FWOOSH!

Zac's bubble was caught in an updraft and he began to drift lazily toward the water below. *Phew!*

Now where's my back-up? Zac wondered. *I thought Leon said —*

THWACK!

Suddenly, an enormous tentacle darted up from the water and caught Zac around the middle, bursting his enormous ParaGum bubble.

'Hey!' Zac shouted out loud.

It looked like some sort of giant octopus or something, except that it was obviously mechanical.

Padded metal tentacles, like the one that had just grabbed Zac, waved in all directions, and…

Suddenly, it dawned on him.

So this is the Squid, Zac thought admiringly.

He had to hand it to his older brother. Leon certainly was creative!

A hatch opened in the top of the Squid. The tentacle holding Zac lowered him inside, where Leon was waiting with the rest of the GIB back-up team.

'Need a lift?' Leon grinned.

'Yeah, thanks,' said Zac. 'Nice ride you've...'

But he trailed off when he saw his parents sitting there.

'What are you doing here?' Zac demanded, as his dad pulled him in for a hug.

'We wanted to make sure you were OK!' his mum replied. 'BIG Central Command! I never thought –'

'I told them you'd be fine,' Leon apologised. 'But they insisted on coming as back-up.'

Zac groaned. *This is so embarrassing!*

'I'm very proud of you,' said Zac's mum, finally releasing him from a hug almost as tight as the Squid's tentacles. 'Now, let's get you home. Don't you think I've forgotten about you sweeping the driveway!'

'But…' Zac began. Surely blowing up BIG's volcano had earned him a bit of time out?

'But nothing,' his mum said sharply. 'You might have saved the world from BIG, but that doesn't mean you get out of doing your chores at home!'

'Fine,' Zac sighed. There were some things even a world-class secret agent couldn't escape.

THE END